Mimmy and Sophie
All Around the Town

Mimmy and Sophie
All Around the Town

Miriam Cohen

Pictures by Thomas F. Yezerski

Frances Foster Books

Farrar, Straus and Giroux
New York

Text copyright © 2004 by Miriam Cohen
Pictures copyright © 2004 by Thomas F. Yezerski
Distributed in Canada by Douglas & McIntyre Ltd.
Printed in the United States of America
Designed by Barbara Grzeslo
First edition, 2004
10 9 8 7 6 5 4 3 2 1

www.fsgkidsbooks.com

Library of Congress Cataloging-in-Publication Data
Cohen, Miriam.
    Mimmy and Sophie all around the town / Miriam Cohen ; pictures
by Thomas F. Yezerski.— 1st ed.
        p. cm.
    Summary: Describes the experiences of two sisters growing up in
Brooklyn in the time of Shirley Temple movies and trolleys.
    ISBN 0-374-34989-4
    [1. Sisters—Fiction.   2. Brooklyn (New York, N.Y.)—Fiction.]
I. Yezerski, Thomas, ill.   II. Title.

PZ7.C6628Mj 2004
[Fic]—dc21

                                                        2003048059

For Frances, of course

—M.C.

To Miriam and Frances

—T.Y.

Contents

In the Alley   1

Coney Island   13

Glory, Glory, Hallelujah!   25

At the Movies   37

Liverwurst Stockings   49

Babyland   61

Mimmy and Sophie
All Around the Town

In the Alley

"Does she always have to tag along?"
Frances said to Mimmy. And Eddy said,
"We're gonna play in the alley. Sophie's too
little."

1

"My mother says I have to take her," Mimmy told the kids. Then they ran down the block to the alley. Sophie tagged along behind.

The alley had good dirt to play in. There were old baby-buggy wheels, tin cans, boards, and bottle caps. You never knew what you could find there.

Eddy said, "I went to the movies Saturday, and I saw *Treasure Island*. Hey, let's dig for pirates' treasure!"

Everybody got sticks and cans to dig with.

Mimmy told Sophie, "Stay out of our way now." So Sophie sat down on Mr. Kelly's back steps and watched.

A big dog that lived in the alley came and sat next to her. Sophie put her arm around its neck.

The kids dug and dug.

"My cousin once found a quarter right on the sidewalk," Lulu said.

"So what? I know this kid that found a shopping bag full of golden jewels," said Eddy.

It was summer in Brooklyn. People fanned themselves. "Boy! It's hot."

At the end of the subway, there was a cool, blue ocean. But that was far away from the alley, like a dream.

"It's too hot to dig for treasure," said Lulu and Frances. But Mimmy and Eddy said, "You'll be sorry when *we* find it."

Lulu's mother brought them a pitcher of purple Kool-Aid with ice cubes in it.

"Yum, I'm drinking wine," said Eddy.

"Ooh!" cried Frances. "I'm gonna tell your mother what you said."

The heat was like a woolly blanket over the alley. Frances stopped digging. Eddy, Mimmy, and Lulu stopped, too.

Then Sophie said, "I know where some treasure is."

"No you don't," said Mimmy.

Sophie got up. She went to a scratchy place under a bush and pointed. "There," said Sophie.

The kids looked at each other. Suddenly everybody began digging and digging.

"There's something here!"

"What is it?"

"It's just an old, rusty oatmeal can."

Eddy shook it. *Bink-a-bank, bink-a-bank* went the can. It sounded like lots of money.

7

"Open it! Hurry up!" the kids cried.

Inside were some tiny toys.

"It's just Cracker Jack prizes. I got a million of them," Eddy said.

"It's still treasure," Mimmy told him.

Lulu and Frances said, "We have to divide it up."

"Sophie gets to pick first," said Mimmy.

"Go ahead, Sophie, you're first," everybody said.

Sophie chose a little baby doll. "Oh! It's the teeniest baby I ever saw." Sophie was so happy.

Mimmy picked a car with a tiny tool set.

Then mothers began calling down the alley, "Come home now! It's getting late!"

When Poppa came home from work, Mimmy and Sophie sat on his lap. Mimmy told him, "You know what, Poppa? Sophie found the treasure."

Poppa smiled. "How did you know where it was, Peanut?"

Sophie whispered in Poppa's ear, "The dog told me."

Coney Island

One Brooklyn summer morning,
Mimmy and Sophie were eating their cereal.

Sophie said, "The little Rice Krispies
boys are saying, 'Nip-nip-nip-nip.' "

"No they're not," said Mimmy. "They
say, 'Snap! Crackle! Pop!' "

"Those Rice Krispies boys are saying, 'Finish your breakfast!' " Poppa said. "This family is going to Coney Island!"

Mimmy and Sophie jumped up and down, they were so happy.

On the trolley, Momma held her little black purse tight. In it was their merry-go-round and frozen custard and hot-dog money.

"We're going on the merry-go-round, we're going on the merry-go-round," sang Sophie.

"*I'm* going on the Whip," said Mimmy.

But Momma's face said, "Oh no you're not."

At last the trolley came to the end of the tracks. So much sky and ocean! Such

14

beautiful Coney Island smells and noise!
Happy people, clackety rides, sweet pink
cotton candy, and the merry-go-round's
music twirling it all around together.

Momma opened the little black purse to
buy hot dogs for each of them. Then she
carefully snapped it shut. Soon everybody
was ready for frozen custard, except Sophie.

"Momma! She's playing with her food!"
cried Mimmy.

15

Sophie was pretending the hot-dog bun
was a little canoe.

They strolled on the boardwalk, eating
delicious frozen custard. The little ocean
waves winked in the sun, and cool breezes
blew. Mimmy stopped to watch a man play
the banjo while a lady tap-danced.

But Sophie was pulling them to the merry-go-round. She ran up to a little white pony with a gold, curly tail and a pink nose. "This one! This one!"

Momma put her on. "Hold tight."

Poppa put Mimmy on a big, strong black horse. Then he and Momma watched Mimmy and Sophie go around.

Sophie held tight to the pole. Up and down. Around and around. She couldn't believe how wonderful it was. Mimmy

spanked her horse to go faster. They both wished the sparkly music would never stop.

When it did, Sophie and Mimmy begged, "One more time, please!"

Momma looked in her little purse. She looked at Poppa. "One more time," she said.

When Momma lifted her off, Sophie kissed her pony on the nose.

Mimmy said, "Why don't you and Poppa take a ride?"

"Oh, no," said Momma. "The merry-go-round is for children and young couples on a date." Then Momma and Poppa went to sit on a bench to look at the ocean.

"We're just going a little way down the boardwalk," Mimmy said. She pulled Sophie by the hand.

"Don't go where we can't see you, now,"
Momma and Poppa said.

Mimmy found two soda cans. She put
them under each of her feet and stamped
down hard.

The soda cans stuck to Mimmy's feet,
and made good tap-dancing shoes. Mimmy
danced and sang, "East Side, West Side, all
around the town!"

Sophie held out a paper cup and
whispered, "East Side, West Side."

"Oh, what a cute little girl," people
said. And they put money in Sophie's
cup.

Mimmy and Sophie ran back to Momma
and Poppa. "Look! *Now* you can go on the
merry-go-round," Mimmy said. "We

danced, and sang a song, and people gave
us free money."

"Oh, Mimmy, that was begging,"
Momma said.

But Poppa said, "Mimmy and Sophie
gave a show for those people, didn't they?

21

That wasn't begging." Then he took
Momma's hand. "Will you go on the
merry-go-round with me, Mrs. Rose
Levinson?"

Mimmy and Sophie waved as Momma
and Poppa went around. Momma was
smiling at Poppa, and Poppa was smiling
at Momma.

"You're on a date! You're on a date!"
cried Mimmy and Sophie.

Glory, Glory, Hallelujah!

Mimmy and Lulu and Frances were playing school on Mimmy's front steps. Eddy was reading his Tarzan comic book.

"Go away, Sophie," Frances said. "We're playing school."

"I can play. I'm almost in kindergarten," said Sophie.

Momma had already bought Sophie new school shoes. They were brown, with laces, and Sophie was learning to tie the bows.

She was going to wear Mimmy's school dress from last year. It was red and green and blue all over. That was called "plaid."

Mimmy and Lulu and Frances put out their pencils and crayons and school notebooks with the speckled covers on the steps. Sophie put her crayon set on the bottom step.

"I'll be Miss Feeney," said Frances. She loved school, and she loved their teacher, Miss Feeney. So did Lulu. But Mimmy

wished Miss Feeney didn't say, "Sit up straight in your seat, Mimmy! How many times do I have to tell you?"

That's why Mimmy liked to sing in the bathtub. "Glory, glory, hallelujah! Teacher hit me with a ruler! So I hit her on the leg with a smelly-rotten egg. Glory, glory, hallelujah!"

"Now," said Frances, "I'm the teacher. Class, did you do your homework?"

"First you have to collect the spelling papers," Lulu said.

"You may collect the spelling papers, Mimmy," Frances said. Then she said, "You have to say, 'Yes, Miss Feeney.'" Mimmy didn't say that, but she collected the

papers. Sophie held out her paper to get it collected.

Frances said, "Why don't you tell her to play with her dolls?"

"Momma wants you, Sophie," Mimmy said.

But Sophie knew Momma was busy sewing.

"Sharpen your pencils, class. We will do our arithmetic."

Mimmy took out her Mickey Mouse pencil sharpener. She could do the numbers, but sometimes her sixes wanted to go the other way, like this—∂.

"Now it's time for our art lesson," said Frances. "Copy this picture and write, 'This is an apple.'" Mimmy took out her twelve-crayon set. It even had a brown crayon and a pink one, for people's faces.

Mimmy decided it was silly to draw an apple. So she drew cars with pink and brown people driving them.

Sophie had a "Little Kid's" set, with six colors. She worked very hard on her

picture. Then she did the words. "Look,
Miss Feeney," she said.

Frances told her, "Sophie, that doesn't
say anything, because you can't write."

"She can't read, either," Lulu said.

"Sophie always bothers us when we're
playing something. She's a pain."

Mimmy was getting mad. "It does *too*
say something! She knows what it says
because she wrote it. Don't you, Sophie?"

Sophie nodded. "Yes."

Eddy looked at Sophie's paper. "It's just
scribble-scrabble," he said. "And the apple
looks like applesauce! Ha, ha! Sophie's not
very smart, I guess."

"Oh!" cried Mimmy. "My father says
Sophie is the smartest little kid in the
whole of Brooklyn! And you're a big
stupid!"

Frances pointed with her pencil at
Mimmy. "Class, go to your seats. That
means Y-O-U!"

"Get off my steps, Miss Bossy Feeney!"
shouted Mimmy. Frances and Lulu took

their pencils and crayons and notebooks.
Eddy took his Tarzan comic book. They
went away down the block.

Mimmy sat on the bottom step with
Sophie. "Hey." Mimmy looked at Sophie's
paper. "This looks just like an 'N.' "

"I know," said Sophie.

At the Movies

Every Saturday, Mimmy and Sophie
went to the Grand Movie Palace. All the
kids on their block did. "Mimmy, take care
of your little sister!" called Momma.

The ticket lady gave Mimmy and Sophie two tickets. She gave them a paper for free glass dishes. Momma was going to get a whole set, with Shirley Temple smiling on every dish. Sophie loved Shirley Temple.

The Grand Movie Palace had the biggest red rug. There was shiny gold everywhere. Looking up, Sophie saw babies with little gold wings flying around heaven. It was beautiful.

Mimmy said to the candy man, "A Baby Ruth, please." She said, "Sophie, hurry up and pick." But Sophie liked to look at all the candy—red Strawberry Twisters, pretty yellow, orange, and green Jujubes, and silver Hershey's Kisses, like hats for little people.

"Hurry up, Sophie! The movie is starting!" Sophie picked Sugar Babies. Mimmy grabbed Sophie's hand and ran after Eddy and Frances and Lulu. They rushed to get seats in the front row. Those were the best. The kids leaned way back and looked up. Shirley Temple was smiling and tap-dancing. Frances said to Mimmy, "My mother said I could take tap-dancing lessons."

"If I take lessons," Mimmy said, "I'm taking drum lessons. Eddy's brother plays the drum like this, 'Bang! Bam!' "

"SHHH! BE QUIET!" the kids behind them shouted.

Sophie whispered, "I have to go to the bathroom."

"Why didn't you go before, when Momma asked you?"

"I didn't have to go then," whispered Sophie.

"In just a minute I'll take you," Mimmy told her.

"I can't wait," whispered Sophie.

Mimmy took Sophie to the ladies' room. "Hurry up, now," said Mimmy. "You're making me miss the movie!"

Many ladies came in and went out of the ladies' room. Lots of people walked around outside. That's how Sophie got lost. She couldn't see Mimmy. Mimmy ran back to the front row. No Sophie!

Mimmy pushed past rows of kids. "Did you see my sister?"

"Who's your sister?"

"She's a little kid, and her name is
Sophie."

"I never heard of her."

"SIT DOWN! I CAN'T SEE!" Some boys
threw popcorn at Mimmy.

A big lady was looking at Sophie. She
had a white dress, and white shoes, and a

flashlight. Sophie knew that lady. She shone
her flashlight at the kids in the dark. She
shouted, "You better stop that noise, you
little monsters!"

"Are you lost?" the big lady asked
Sophie.

Sophie shook her head. "No."

"What's your name?"

"Sophie."

"What's your mother and father's name?"

"Momma and Poppa."

"You're lost, girlie," said the lady. Big tears came into Sophie's eyes.

The lady went up and down the theater with Sophie. "Did anyone lose a little kid?"

"Sophie!" Mimmy came running. She told Sophie, "You're going to get a good spanking! You're just trying to get me in trouble!"

Sophie hid her face against Mimmy's dress, and cried. Then Mimmy began to cry, she was so glad to see Sophie!

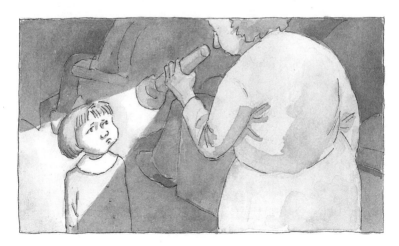

Mimmy took Sophie back to their seats. She fixed Sophie's hair bow, and whispered, "Eat your Sugar Babies." Then Mimmy put her arm around Sophie, and they watched Shirley Temple. Shirley was smiling and tap-dancing and singing, all at the same time.

Liverwurst Stockings

"But, Momma! It's spring already,"
Mimmy cried. "Why do we still have to
wear our winter stockings?"

And Sophie said, "A dog might eat our
stockings. He might think they are
liverwurst."

"I don't want you to catch a cold," Momma told them. "Go outside and play now."

Mimmy and Sophie stayed in the alley so nobody would see their liverwurst stockings.

Kids played marbles and jump-rope on their block. Girls had on short socks and Mary Jane shoes. Boys had sneakers.

"*Nobody* is still wearing winter stockings and high shoes," said Mimmy.

"Come on!" Mimmy helped Sophie through the hole in their fence.

On the other side was a big, empty lot. Mimmy and Sophie were really not supposed to play there, because they would

get too dirty. Then Momma would have to do more laundry in the big tub.

The lot had little roads all over. Kids'

sneakers had made them. It had tall cattails, and spring puddle-lakes.

"This is Florida," said Mimmy. "And that's the ocean."

"Here," Mimmy said. "Help me put this board across so we can go over the ocean, to Florida."

Sophie lifted up one end, but it was too heavy. The board fell right into the ocean, and a big wave came up and splashed her.

Sophie's dress and stockings were all wet and muddy. Sophie looked scared. "Momma's going to be mad."

But Mimmy went stomping into the middle of the mud puddle. She jumped up and down. "It's spring! Hooray!"

Sophie began to paddle in the muddy water. "I like it. It feels nice," she said.

Mimmy threw bigger and bigger rocks to make bigger and bigger splashes.

"Mimmy and Sophie! Come home for lunch now!" Momma was calling from the kitchen window.

Mimmy and Sophie stopped playing. They looked at each other.

They walked very slowly down the alley and up the front steps.

"Miriam Sarah!" Momma said, because Mimmy was bigger, and should know better.

Momma looked A LONG LOOK at Mimmy and Sophie. Sophie began to cry.

Momma filled up the tub. Then she took their clothes and shoes away.

Mimmy helped Sophie get washed.
Then she washed herself. They were very
quiet.

Momma came back with clean clothes.
Still she didn't say a word. She put Sophie's
underwear on and pulled Sophie's dress over
her head.

Then Momma began to put socks on Sophie's feet—little, white springtime socks! And Mary Jane shoes! She had bigger socks for Mimmy, and Mimmy's sneakers. Mimmy could run faster and push her skate-box better with sneakers.

Mimmy and Sophie went outside. "Oh, boy! Watch how fast I can run now!" Mimmy raced down the block.

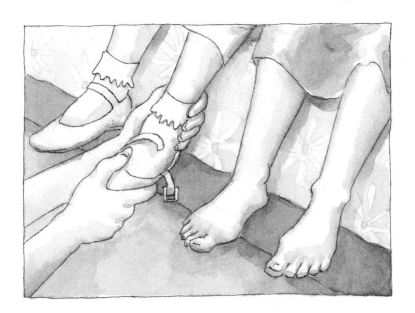

Sophie sat on the steps. She looked at
her shiny Mary Janes, and her white socks
with ruffles on them.

Little breezes blew. The sun shone.

The sky was shining like Momma's
windows after she polished them. Brooklyn
shone. It was spring.

Babyland

Mimmy was riding her skate-box in their alley. Sophie played with her five dolly babies.

"Do you know what?" Sophie said. "I went to Babyland."

"No you didn't!" said Mimmy. "When you're as old as me, you'll know there's *no* Babyland."

"Yes, there is, because I went there," Sophie said. "Babyland is *way* downtown. I went on the bus . . ."

But Mimmy said, "You didn't have money for the bus."

"I went with a nice lady that had lots of little children.

"Then we got on the train—"

"You can't even read," Mimmy said. "How did you know where to get off?"

"I just got off when the lady did. And it was downtown.

"And then I walked for a long, long time. And then I saw a beautiful place, with lights, and it had a picture on it of all the little babies.

"So I opened the door, and it looked just like heaven! And I went inside and played with the little babies, and I gave them their bottles and everything."

"When you are as old as me," Mimmy said, "you won't tell silly stories." And she skated away on her skate-box.

"Could she *really* go downtown by herself?" Mimmy wondered. She came around the block and stopped in front of Sophie. "Where did you get the idea of Babyland?"

"Oh, I *always* knew about it. And I heard Uncle Walter tell Momma and Poppa that he went there," said Sophie.

Mimmy went around the block again.

This time she jumped off her skate-box, and went up the steps into the house.

"Momma, Sophie says she went downtown by herself to Babyland. She says she heard Uncle Walter tell about it when he was here."

"My goodness!" said Momma. "Uncle Walter told us he went downtown to *Gravyland*, the famous restaurant."

"Ah-ha!" cried Mimmy, and she ran outside. She was going to say to Sophie,

"See! I told you there isn't any Babyland. Uncle Walter said he went downtown to *Gravyland*."

Sophie was taking her five baby dollies for a ride in a little baby buggy.

"Hey!" said Mimmy.

"What?" said Sophie.

"Want me to take you for a ride on my skate-box?"

"Oh, yes! Can I bring my babies?"

"Sure," Mimmy said. "Hold on tight."

AR 2.9
Pts 0.5

IX
8/12